MOLLY PATCH
and
Her Animal Friends

BY BEN SHECTER

HARPER & ROW, PUBLISHERS
New York   Evanston
San Francisco   London

For Ollie and Jem

Molly Patch And Her Animal Friends
Copyright © 1975 by Ben Shecter
Printed in the U.S.A. All rights reserved.
Library of Congress Catalog Card Number: 75–6304
Trade Standard Book Number: 06–025586–2
Harpercrest Standard Book Number: 06–025589–7
First Edition

STORIES

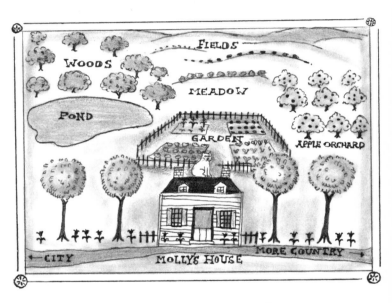

This is a map to Molly's house.

When the city noises grew too loud, and friendly faces disappeared, Molly Patch moved to the country. At first Molly didn't know anyone. She busied herself with her plants, cooking, and writing in her notebook.

Molly also spent a lot of time just looking at things inside and outside her house. One day when Molly was out looking at the wild flowers, she came across Raccoon, who appeared to be ill. His eyes were watery and his nose was dry, and when Molly pressed her lips against his head she cried, "This poor Raccoon has a fever!"

Molly took Raccoon to her house and put him to bed. She fed him hot soup and gave him plenty of tea with toast and jam. After the fever was gone, Molly hugged Raccoon and said, "I'm so glad you're getting better."

On the day Raccoon was feeling perfectly well again and it was time for him to leave, he hugged Molly and thanked her for all she had done.

Molly Patch hugged Raccoon and said, "It was my pleasure!"

Raccoon told all the animals about Molly Patch. "She fed me jams and jellies, and she hugs a lot too!" he said.

A few days later, Molly Patch found Mole at her doorstep, moaning and groaning.

"I'm sick," he cried.

"You poor dear," said Molly, and she carried Mole into her house. Her treatment for Mole was the same as it was for Raccoon. Only Mole told Molly Patch that he liked peach jam the best.

The day after Mole left, Bear knocked on Molly's door. "Hello. I'm not feeling too well," he said.

"Oh, that's too bad," said Molly Patch. "What seems to be the trouble?"

"Well, I just hurt all over," said Bear.

Molly invited Bear in, and she gave him plenty of tea with honey and lots of hugs.

"I feel great now," said Bear. He thanked Molly and left.

On the days that followed, Molly was visited by

other animals, all saying they were sick. Molly's treatment for all of them was the same.

One sunny afternoon when Molly was picnicking in the meadow, she was suddenly surrounded by the animals. They were all moaning, groaning, rolling on the ground, and crying that they were sick.

Molly shook her head and laughed. "You all look perfectly well to me," she said.

"We do?" they cried.

3

"We're all sick," coughed Bear.

"That was a fake cough if I ever heard one," said Molly.

"Really?" said Bear. "I thought it was quite good."

Molly opened her picnic basket. "You don't have to pretend you're sick," she said. "You're all welcome to my food anytime."

"And your hugs, too?" asked Mole.

Molly Patch smiled and said, "My hugs too!" Then she gave all the animals jelly sandwiches and she hugged them.

A Page From Molly's Notebook

you'd think the
field folks'
chattering
would stop
when the day's at end
but there's night talk too,
listen

A SKATING LESSON

Wintertime settled along the canal. Rooftops sagged under the snow, and woodpiles grew small. Molly Patch spent her time reading and sewing.

One day Molly was visited by Field Mouse, who asked her if she wanted to go ice-skating.

Molly said, "I don't have time for things like that."

"Find the time," said Field Mouse. "It's good for you!"

"No, thank you," said Molly. "I know what's good for me." She went back to sewing her quilt.

A few days later Field Mouse visited Molly again.

"How are you today?" he asked.

"Fine," said Molly.

Field Mouse looked at Molly. "You don't look fine," he said.

"I don't?" cried Molly, and she ran to the mirror.

"I hope you feel better," said Field Mouse, and he left.

For days, Molly sat in front of the mirror worrying about how she looked. After a while she began to feel awful.

When Field Mouse came by again and asked Molly how she felt, Molly answered, "Not too well."

"What you need is some outdoor exercise," said Field Mouse.

"What did you have in mind?" asked Molly.

"Ice-skating, of course," said Field Mouse. He whirled around the room pretending he was skating.

"Have a good time on the ice today," said Molly, and she reached for her sewing basket.

"Aren't you coming with me?" asked Field Mouse.

"I'd really like to," said Molly, "but I don't have any ice skates."

"I know where you can get a pair," said Field Mouse.

"Anyway, I just remembered something," cried Molly. "I've got to stay home and bake a pie."

"No you don't," said Field Mouse. "You can

have the one I baked this morning."

"What kind is it?" asked Molly.

"Blueberry," said Field Mouse.

"I don't like blueberry pie," said Molly.

"Since when?" asked Field Mouse.

"Since I don't want to go skating," said Molly.

"Why not?" asked Field Mouse.

"Because I don't know how to skate and everyone is going to laugh at me!" cried Molly.

"No one is going to laugh," said Field Mouse.

"Are you sure?" asked Molly.

"Certainly!" said Field Mouse. "I'd never laugh."

"All right, then," sighed Molly. "I'll go!"

On the way to the canal they stopped at Owl's Thrift Shop. There Molly got her skates.

The canal was crowded with skaters. Field Mouse helped Raccoon lace up Molly's skates.

Molly stood up on wobbly legs. "I'll never be able to skate!" she cried.

"Stop being silly!" said Field Mouse, and he led Molly onto the ice.

"Watch me," said Field Mouse. "One, two,

three, glide." Field Mouse moved easily across the ice, and then stood on the bank to watch Molly.

"One, t-w-o-o-o, t-h-r-e-e, OOOOOOPPPSSS!" cried Molly, and she fell.

Field Mouse laughed. Molly remained seated on the ice, and she took off her skates. Then she got up and left.

"Wait, Molly Patch!" shouted Field Mouse. But Molly hurried home.

At home Molly took up her sewing again. That afternoon, when Porcupine came by to deliver the newspapers, Molly invited him in for some hot soup.

Porcupine finished his soup and watched Molly work on her patchwork quilt. "That looks hard," he said.

"It isn't so hard once you learn how to do it," said Molly.

"I suppose that's the way it is with most things," said Porcupine. He thanked Molly for the soup and left.

For the rest of that day and all through the night, Molly could think of nothing else but skating.

Early the next morning, before breakfast, Molly went to the canal. She was the only one there. Molly put on her skates and laced them tightly. Then she stepped onto the ice.

"One, two, three," said Molly.

"Glide!" shouted Field Mouse.

Molly was surprised by Field Mouse. "What are you doing here so early in the morning?" she asked.

"Looking for you," said Field Mouse.

"For me?" cried Molly. "How did you know I'd be here?"

"When I went to your house this morning to apologize and you weren't there, I figured you'd be here," said Field Mouse.

"How come?" said Molly.

"Because I did the same thing when I began to skate. Only it was my sister who laughed when I fell."

Slowly, Molly began to glide around the ice.

"That's it!" shouted Field Mouse. "Just tell yourself that you're wonderful."

"I'm wonderful! I'm wonderful! I'm wonderful!"

"Let's not overdo it," said Field Mouse.

Molly took a big glide and fell. She looked at Field Mouse and began to laugh. Field Mouse laughed too.

A Page From Molly's Notebook

the
 wind
  pulls
   the smoke
    from the chimney
snow settles on the tall black pines
soon it will be another year

A SONG FOR BEAR

Molly Patch picked some violets and placed them in a cup on the mantel. Then she cleaned the soot from the chimney and the ashes from the fireplace.

"Bear will be waking soon," she said.

On the morning Molly changed her winter quilt for a spring one, she went to call on Bear. She took along some pastries.

At Bear's, the curtains were drawn and the door was closed. "I guess he's still sleeping," Molly said. But she decided to wait.

Crow came by. "What are you waiting for?" he asked Molly.

"I'm waiting for Bear to wake up," said Molly. "I want to welcome him back after his long sleep."

"That sounds nice," said Crow. "Do you mind if I wait with you?"

Molly told Crow that she didn't mind at all. "I'm sure Bear will be happy to see you."

Raccoon saw Molly and Crow, and he joined them. "Looks like you're waiting for something," said Raccoon.

"We are," they said. "We're waiting to greet Bear when he wakes."

Raccoon looked at Bear's house. "How come he isn't up yet?" he asked.

"Bear's not very good about time," said Molly.

"I'll wait with you," said Raccoon. "It will be good to see Bear again."

Chicken and Goose passed Bear's house on their way from the market. "What's happening?" they asked.

"We're waiting for Bear to get up," said Molly.

"If you don't mind, we'll wait also," they said.

"I'm sure Bear will be happy to see us when he wakes," said Molly.

It didn't take long for Bear to appear at his window. When he did, he rubbed his eyes.

"Happy waking!" they shouted.

Bear disappeared.

"He's going to open the door," said Molly.

But after a while when the door didn't open, Chicken said, "Do you think he's gone back to sleep again?"

Rabbit came by. He was surprised to hear about Bear's strange behavior.

"Maybe he's grumpy," said Rabbit. "I'm always grumpy when I get up."

"Perhaps if we sing him a nice spring song, he will open his door," said Crow.

"It's an idea," they said. So they all sang a song.

Wake up, wake up
for the greening of spring.
Wake up, wake up,
can't you hear us sing?

When they finished, Bear still didn't open his door. But they felt that they all sang so well together they should form a glee club.

"I wonder what he's doing," said Goose.

"Bear, I've brought you some pastries," said Molly.

Everyone was sure that Bear would come to the door for Molly's pastries. Still there wasn't any sign of him.

"Maybe he doesn't like pastries," said Raccoon.

Chicken and Goose looked in their marketing baskets.

"Bear, I've got elderberries, sweet cream, and cinnamon rolls," said Chicken.

14

"And I've got cheese, raisins, and maple syrup," said Goose.

There still wasn't any response from Bear.

But they all licked their lips and rubbed their stomachs.

"We can have a party," said Raccoon.

They agreed it was a good idea to have a party.

"Bear is sure to join us," said Molly.

Raccoon told jokes. Crow whistled and Rabbit performed magic tricks. Then they played games, and after the game playing they ate.

The last pastry disappeared and there wasn't any sign of Bear. When the sun turned red and was about to leave the sky, the party ended. They all said good-bye and told each other what a good time they had.

Molly Patch stayed behind, cleaning up. When she finished and was about to leave, Bear appeared at the door.

"Happy spring," said Molly.

"Happy spring to you," said Bear.

"Why didn't you come out when you got up?" asked Molly.

"I had to go back and finish a dream," said Bear.
"We had a good party," said Molly.
"I had a very good dream," said Bear.
Sweet spring smells drifted in with the darkness. Bear told Molly about his dream.

A Page From Molly's Notebook

springtime
dreams
colored
buttercup
lilac
and
tulip pink

THE DREAM

"You were in my dream," said Bear.

"I was?" said Molly Patch.

Bear shook his head yes. "At the beginning part, anyway," he said.

Molly was surprised to hear that she had been a part of Bear's dream. "What did I do in it?" asked Molly.

Bear closed his eyes, remembering. "The dream began with you building a new house."

Molly laughed. "That sounds like the start of quite a dream."

"No laughing," said Bear. "Or I won't tell you the dream."

"Okay, I promise, no laughing," said Molly Patch. "Even if it is funny."

"You can laugh at the funny parts," said Bear.

"What if I laugh at something I think is funny and you don't?" asked Molly Patch.

A puzzled look came upon Bear's face. "Oh, all right, you can laugh at anything you want to."

"Oh, good!" sighed Molly. "I hate to hold back a laugh; it hurts so much."

Molly Patch rested against a fallen bough and listened as Bear told his dream.

"It was a terrific spring day. The kind of day when the smell of lilacs almost makes you feel silly. I was walking through the woods when I heard a hammering sound. At first I thought it was old Woodpecker, but when I really listened, I knew it wasn't him. You can imagine how surprised I was when I discovered it was you building a great, big, new house."

"Imagine that," sighed Molly.

"Oh, Molly, you should have seen your house. It was really something special!"

"Was it like a castle?" asked Molly Patch.

"Not exactly," said Bear.

Molly sighed with disappointment.

"It was better than a castle," said Bear.

"It was?" cried Molly.

"It was such a beautiful house that I decided it was time for me to have a big new house also. Well, you know in dreams anything is possible, so I

19

quickly found the perfect spot for my house. It was in the middle of a flower-filled meadow. Honey-bees swarmed all over the place. And they had their hives right nearby. Can you imagine that? The entire meadow was just dripping with honey. Oh, Molly, it was a wonderful spot.

"Then I began to build my house. It was big and it looked perfect. My dream was interrupted at that part. That's when I got up and went to the window. You can see why I didn't go out and join you. I just had to go back and finish the dream."

Molly Patch nodded and rested her head on a mossy pillow.

"When I went back to sleep, my house had grown, and there were even more flowers and bees in the meadow. I went inside the house through a huge front door. And inside, it was just the grandest place I'd ever seen. There were rooms, hallways, stairways, and more rooms. There were so many rooms that I got lost." Bear laughed.

"It seems funny now," said Bear. "While I was dreaming it, I was a little scared. I don't like being lost."

"No one does," said Molly.

Bear sighed and continued. "The one strange thing about the house was that there weren't any windows or doors. I went from room to room, hallway to stairway, and back to rooms again, looking for a way out. And when it seemed like there wasn't any way out at all, I heard some noise. It was chattering sounds. In one room I discovered some trolls having a party.

"I had never seen trolls like them before. I remember being annoyed, and I said, 'What are you doing in my house?'

"They all laughed at me. Well, that really made me angry, and I said, 'Get out of my house!' But they continued to laugh. I finally said, 'What's so funny?'

"They wrote me a note, and it said, WE DON'T UNDERSTAND A WORD YOU'RE SAYING.

"I said, 'What *do* you understand?'

"And then they wrote me another note, and it said, WE ONLY UNDERSTAND NOTES.

"So after a lot of note passing, I discovered that

I had built my house over theirs. I must say they were nice about it, because they invited me to their party. And I had the most delicious honey-flavored ice cream with cookies.

"Then they wrote a note. It said,

Wake up, wake up
for the greening of spring.
Wake up, wake up,
can't you hear us sing?

"When I read the note, I could almost hear it being sung. After that, they showed me the way out. The funny thing was that the way out took me right into my very own house. That's when I woke up. What do you think of that dream?" said Bear.

Molly Patch was fast asleep.

"I hope you're having a good dream," whispered Bear.

Bear looked at his house and up at the sky. The stars seemed brighter than he remembered them. He laughed softly, happy to be awake again after his long winter sleep.

Molly Patch rubbed her eyes and shook some mossy ribbons from her hair. She smiled and said, "Let's look at the stars together."

"Yes," said Bear, "it's more fun that way."

Molly Patch and Bear sat up all the night wondering how many stars there were.

A Page From Molly's Notebook

Bear
and I
count
the stars
and before
we're
through
it's morning

DEAR TOAD

When Molly Patch lived in the city, she had to shop for her vegetables and flowers. But in the country she had a terrific garden. Vegetables, herbs, and flowers grew alongside each other. Molly spent a lot of time in her garden.

One day Molly found Toad in her sweet Williams. She was watering when Toad said, "More water, please."

Molly sprinkled more water. Toad giggled. "This is the best shower I've ever had."

"I'm glad," said Molly.

"Would you like me to give you a shower?" asked Toad.

"No, thank you," said Molly. "I prefer baths."

Toad wandered through the flowers, sniffing at the delphiniums. "I like your garden," he said.

"You may stay here if you like," said Molly.

Toad jumped up and down. "Oh, yes!" he shouted.

Molly made a gardening apron just like hers for

Toad. At first Toad was embarrassed to wear it. But when Molly said, "An apron is an apron," Toad put it on. He pretended it didn't have ruffles and daisies on it.

Molly and Toad began to work in the garden together. One morning, Molly said, "Today we are going to prune."

Toad made a face. "What's the matter?" asked Molly. "Don't you feel well?"

"I feel well," said Toad. "I don't like prunes."

Molly laughed. "Pruning means to trim. We are just going to cut back the suckers from the tomato plants."

"I didn't see anyone sucking on the tomato plants," said Toad.

"No, no!" said Molly. "Suckers are the extra leaves on the tomato plant. They prevent the tomatoes from growing big and healthy."

Together they trimmed the tomato plants.

"Now we've got to put stakes in the ground for the tomatoes," said Molly.

Toad looked puzzled. "I didn't know tomatoes liked steak."

Molly laughed loudly. "No, no. Wooden stakes, to support the tomato plants, or else they will topple and fall to the ground."

After all the stakes were in the ground, Molly and Toad tore narrow strips of cloth and carefully tied the tomato plants to the wooden stakes.

When they finished, Molly said, "Now they will grow well, thanks to your help, dear Toad."

Toad smiled proudly. That night, Toad scrubbed Molly's back and sang to her. Molly hummed along. After her bath, Molly made spinach pie and asparagus pudding.

Toad didn't like spinach pie, but he ate it anyway because he liked Molly.

One warm afternoon when it was shower time, Molly called Toad. But he didn't answer. "Are you playing games, Toad?" she asked. But when she called again and he still didn't answer, Molly grew worried.

She searched through the garden, looking under the cabbage leaves and through the tangle of nasturtiums. But all she found were some ladybugs and Mole.

When Molly asked Mole if he had seen Toad, he burped and answered, "No."

"You've been in my peppers," scolded Molly.

"How did you know?" said Mole, feeling ashamed.

"Your burp gave you away," said Molly.

"Peppers just don't agree with me," sighed Mole, and he burped again.

Molly continued her search through the cucumber vines, and there she came across Snake, who was looking very fat.

"Have you seen Toad?" asked Molly.

Snake looked up at Molly lazily. "I've not only seen Toad," he said, "I've eaten him."

"Eaten him!" cried Molly.

Snake smiled.

"Give him back to me," said Molly.

"No," said Snake.

"How could you do a thing like that?" asked Molly.

"I was hungry," said Snake.

"There are other things to eat besides Toad," said Molly.

"But I like Toad," said Snake.

"I love Toad," said Molly. "Please return him," she begged.

"Then what will I eat?" said Snake.

"Anything but Toad," said Molly.

"Anything isn't as good as Toad," said Snake. And he began to wriggle away.

Molly got angry. "Return him, or I'll hit you over the head with the hoe!" she cried.

Snake remained silent.

"Hoes can hurt," said Molly.

Snake opened his mouth wide, and Toad jumped out.

Molly kissed Toad and said, "I'm glad to see you again."

Toad kissed Molly back and said, "I'm glad to see you too!"

Molly looked at Snake. "I'll give you something else to eat," she said.

"What?" said Snake.

"It will be a surprise," said Molly.

"I hate surprises," said Snake. "What are you going to give me?"

"Nothing at all," said Molly, "if you won't accept my surprise."

"Well, I guess a surprise is better than nothing," said Snake, and he decided to wait.

Molly's surprise was strawberry doughnuts. Toad made iced tea. And they had a garden party.

"These doughnuts are good," said Toad.

"They *are* good," said Molly, "if I must say so myself."

Snake ate his doughnut slowly. "It *is* good," he said. "Almost as good as Toad."

The glee club out rehearsing stopped by. Molly offered them things to eat. Afterward, Molly, Toad, and Snake joined the group, singing songs. They sang about the joys of food.

Snake said he was getting hungry again, and Molly put another doughnut in his mouth.

A Page From Molly's Notebook

little brown Toad
hidden in the clover
didn't you know Snake was watching?

A SPECIAL NAME

One rainy morning Mole went to visit Molly Patch.

"Perfect timing," said Molly Patch. "I just took some raisin cookies out of the oven."

Mole took one, nibbled at it, and then put it down.

"Aren't they any good?" asked Molly, tasting one herself.

"Sure," said Mole. "I'm not hungry."

Molly looked at Mole. "What's the matter?" she asked.

"I'm tired of just being called Mole," he said.

"But that's who you are," said Molly.

"I know," said Mole. "But I want to be called by a special name."

"What would you like your name to be?" asked Molly.

"I haven't decided yet," said Mole. "I'm still at the thinking point. I thought you might have some ideas."

"I always thought Mole sounded so nice. It

would be difficult for me to think of any other name for you," said Molly.

"Thanks for the cookie," said Mole, and he left.

Mole sat beneath the potted ferns near Molly's door. He watched the rain and thought of important-sounding names: names like Cloudburst, Thunder, and Lightning. He said them aloud, but none of them seemed like the right name.

When the rain stopped, Mole walked to the meadow. He followed the stone fence to where the big oak tree interrupted it and made a shadow the size of the pond. Mole felt very small beneath the big tree. And it was there that he decided to call himself Oak Tree.

"That sounds really important," he told himself.

Returning home, Mole saw Raccoon posting a notice. It read:

PLAYWRITING CONTEST
The winning play will receive a
first-class production.
All entries must be sent to Raccoon,
Director of the Apple Orchard Players.

Mole read the notice. When he got home, he decided to enter the contest. "I'll write an important play to go with my new name," he said.

Mole walked around for days, trying to think about important things. He finally decided to write a play about a king.

The night-lights glowed steadily at Mole's while he worked on his play. And when it was finished, he called it *The Brave King*. He signed his name Oak Tree.

It grew difficult for Mole to think about anything but the contest. Finally, the day arrived when they announced the winning play. Mole rushed to the posted notice. There was a crowd around it, mumbling.

"Who won? Who won?" asked Mole, unable to read the notice because of the crowd.

"No one we've ever heard of," said Rabbit.

"Someone named Oak Tree," said Goose.

"That's me!" shouted Mole.

Everyone laughed. "You're Mole!" they cried.

"No, I'm Mole Oak Tree. I just changed my name."

But everyone continued laughing.

Mole was unhappy. He went to visit Molly Patch.

"Oh dear," cried Molly. "I've never seen such gloom. What's the matter?"

Mole told Molly what had happened. And when he finished, he had to borrow Molly's handkerchief to wipe away a few tears.

"Poor Mole," said Molly. "Come with me and we'll get this situation straightened out."

Molly took Mole to Raccoon's. There she explained what had happened.

"Why didn't you sign your real name?" asked Raccoon.

"Because I thought Oak Tree sounded more important," Mole sighed.

"It's who you are and what you do that's important," said Molly.

Mole shook his head in agreement.

A new announcement was posted, and everyone congratulated Mole on winning the playwriting contest.

Molly helped him celebrate by baking a big fudge cake with the name MOLE written across the top in vanilla icing.

A Page From Molly's Notebook

He looks like Mole
I think it's him
I call his name
He doesn't answer
Does Mole know
who Mole is?

THE BRAVE KING

The Apple Orchard Players posted casting notices for their new play. Bear read the notice.

**Wanted: Able actors and actresses for the play
THE BRAVE KING
Someone big wanted for the part of the king
Someone not so big wanted for the queen
And all different sizes for the other parts**

Bear decided to try out. He went to the apple orchard, where the other animals were waiting to audition.

Raccoon, the play's director, said Bear could have the part of the king because he was bigger than anyone else. And Chicken got the part of the queen because everyone thought she looked regal. Rabbit, Fox, and Field Mouse were cast in other parts.

Rehearsals began, and Raccoon told Bear to get into the spirit of things. "Pretend you are a king," he said.

Molly Patch designed the costumes for the play.

After the costumes were made, Bear wore his crown and robe all the time.

Raccoon visited Bear. "How is my loyal subject?" asked Bear.

Raccoon laughed. "That sounds good," he said. "You're really into the part."

"Into the part?" said Bear. "I *am* the part!"

In the days that followed, Bear greeted everyone the same way, calling them his loyal subjects. They all laughed.

Bear learned his lines and went about shouting, "I am the bravest king in the land!"

When Raccoon visited Bear again, he noticed that Bear had replaced his old rocking chair with a throne. When Raccoon asked him why he did that, Bear answered, "My dear subject, don't you know that thrones are for kings?"

As the play rehearsals continued, Bear wouldn't listen to Raccoon, the director. One day Bear said, "No one tells a king what to do!" And he walked away.

"We can't have our play, *The Brave King*, without a king," Mole told Molly Patch.

The play rehearsals stopped. Everyone was sad.

But when anyone wanted to see Bear and talk to him, he just said, "The king is seeing no one." At last the animals stopped knocking on Bear's door. For days Bear sat alone on his throne.

The longer Bear remained at home playing king by himself, the lonelier he got. "It just isn't any fun being a king with no one around," said Bear.

He put away his crown and cape, got off his throne, and went to visit Molly.

When he knocked on her door, and she said, "Who's there?" he answered, "Bear."

And when Molly said, "King Bear?" he answered, "No, just Bear Bear."

"That's good," said Molly, opening the door. "Because I didn't feel like entertaining royalty today."

Bear laughed and said he was sorry for being so silly.

Molly spoke to Bear about the play. Bear said that he would be happy to return to playing the part of the king again.

"But only on stage," Molly warned.

Bear nodded in agreement.

The play was a great success, and everyone said that Bear made a very good brave king.

Molly told Bear that he was a very good actor.

A Page From Molly's Notebook

the curtain
goes up
on a room
in a castle
there's a
king and queen
who are noble and brave
it's only parts
they're
playing

THE LONG SLEEP

There were still some leaves on the trees when it began to snow. Bear watched the snowflakes drift down from the chimney into the fireplace. "It must be time for my winter sleep," he said.

Bear got his house in order and went to bed. He yawned and told himself that he was sleepy. But he couldn't fall asleep. He tossed and turned and tried to think about nice things to make him sleepy.

He thought about spring meadows, wild berries, and swarms of bees. And then he thought about honey, and he got hungry. Bear got up and treated himself to cookies, jam, and warm milk. "Now I'll sleep," he said.

In bed, he covered himself with a big woolly blanket and tried to find a comfortable position. Just as he settled down, there was a knock on the door.

"I'm so glad you're here," said Goose. "It's getting a bit chilly and I don't have any firewood."

"You can have all of mine," said Bear. "I won't

be needing it. I'm going to sleep for the winter."

"Pleasant dreams," said Goose, and she left with all of Bear's firewood.

Bear got back into bed and searched for a good sleeping position. In searching for one, he got tangled in his big woolly blanket and fell to the floor.

When Bear finally got settled in bed again, there was another knock on the door.

Bear pulled the blanket over his head and pretended he wasn't at home. The knocking continued, and unable to ignore it any longer, Bear went to the door.

At the door was Rabbit. "I hope I'm not disturbing you," said Rabbit.

"Oh no," said Bear, trying to be polite.

"Would you like some preserves for the winter?" asked Rabbit.

"No thank you," said Bear. "I hope I will sleep through the winter."

Rabbit wished him a good sleep and left.

Bear looked at his bed. He stretched, yawned, and climbed into it. "I'm sleepy, I'm sleepy, I'm sleepy!" he told himself. He put his head down on the pillow, and the pillow seemed hard. The woolly blanket seemed too warm, and the bed began to creak.

Bear jumped out of bed and walked around the room. After a while he heard a tapping on the window. It was Molly Patch.

Bear opened the window. "Hello Molly," he said unhappily.

"What's the trouble?" asked Molly Patch.

Bear told Molly about his problem. "It's winter, and I've got to sleep," he said.

"Perhaps it isn't your sleeping time yet," said Molly.

Bear looked at Molly, surprised.

"Let me in and I'll read to you," said Molly Patch.

"Read to me?" said Bear. "I don't want to hear any stories. I want to sleep."

"That's how my mother got me to sleep when I was little," said Molly.

"Oh, well, I hope it works," said Bear. He let Molly in and returned to bed.

"What kind of story shall I read you?" asked Molly.

"The kind that will put me right to sleep," said Bear.

Molly Patch took a book down from the shelf. It was a book about basket weaving, and it didn't take long before Molly fell asleep herself.

Bear listened to Molly snore. He got out of bed. The house had grown cold. Bear went outside to gather firewood.

While Bear was out, Molly woke up. When she discovered Bear gone, she searched the house for him. She even looked under the bed.

"What are you looking for?" asked Bear.

"I was looking for you," said Molly.

"The story didn't work," said Bear.

"I'm sorry," said Molly. "But I had a delightful sleep!"

"With delightful snoring," said Bear.

Bear made a fire and invited Molly to stay for dinner. After dinner, Bear and Molly sat in front of the fireplace.

Outside, it seemed as if winter had happened all at once. The canal froze over and an icy wind raced around the house. The grandfather clock chimed.

"It's late. Time for me to go home and really

sleep," said Molly. She turned to Bear. Bear's eyes were almost closed.

"I guess it's time for you, too," whispered Molly, and she helped Bear to bed.

"Good winter," said Molly Patch. "I'll see you in the spring."

Molly put out the fire and quietly closed the door as she left.

A Page From Molly's Notebook

> sleep
> gentle Bear
> the winter
> is long
> we'll wake you
> again
> with a
> sweet spring song

Plants grew well at Molly Patch's house—so well that when her friends visited, they complained that there wasn't any room for them.

When the animals got together, they would talk about the plant situation at Molly's.

"I had to share my seat with a geranium," said Goose.

"And I got tickled on the nose by the ivy," said Raccoon.

"The spider plant crawled into my lemonade," cried Chicken.

When Bear visited Molly after his winter sleep, he was surprised to see how her plants had grown —and multiplied.

"Why don't you give some of them away?" he said.

But Molly said, "Never. I love them all!"

The day Molly Patch left for the spring flower show, her friends gathered to say good-bye and wish her luck. She was entering her prized gardenia in the show.

Molly gave her friends plant-watering instructions. "The asparagus fern needs very little watering, the Boston fern needs more, and the cactus can go without any until I return. A moderate amount for the others."

"It's all so confusing," murmured Chicken.

Molly Patch waved good-bye and disappeared down the road.

On plant-watering day, the animals gathered at Molly's.

"By the time we finish watering the last plant," moaned Field Mouse, "we'll have to start all over again."

The animals filled their watering cans and began their task.

"There are begonias in the bed," shouted Bear.

"And violets in the kitchen sink," said Fox.

"Not to mention the coleus on the potty," sighed Chicken.

Goose sat down exhausted. "We've got to help Molly," she said. "Soon there won't be any room for her inside this house."

"Poor Molly will have to live outside," cried Field Mouse.

Bear paced up and down. "I have an idea," he said. "The plants will live outside the house and Molly will still be able to enjoy them all year long."

"How is that possible?" asked Chicken.

"We will build a greenhouse for Molly," said Bear.

Everyone agreed that it was a good idea.

"What shall it look like?" asked Raccoon.

"Why don't we each design a greenhouse?" said Bear. "And we'll vote on the best one and then build it."

That night, all the animals drew pictures of what they thought the greenhouse should look like.

In the morning it was decided that they would combine the designs of Bear, Fox, and Chicken.

Goose objected; she said she didn't like anything about Chicken's design.

Chicken said, "What does a silly goose like you know about greenhouses?"

Chicken and Goose had a big argument as to who knew more about greenhouses.

Bear told them to stop arguing. "Let's get to work," he said.

The animals worked hard, hoping to finish the greenhouse before Molly's return.

Goose and Chicken worked side by side, but they didn't speak to each other.

"Friends shouldn't quarrel," said Field Mouse.

"We're not friends," they said.

After the last pane of glass had been put in its place, the animals complimented each other on

the fine-looking greenhouse they had built.

"I hope Molly likes it," said Field Mouse.

"We'll know soon enough," said Bear. "Molly should be returning tonight."

Then they formed a chain and brought all of the plants into the greenhouse. Chicken almost dropped the cactus. "It hurts!" she cried.

The animals wanted to stay awake for Molly's return, but they were just too tired, and they all went home to sleep.

Molly Patch returned late that night, and when she discovered her plants gone, she dropped her prize-winning gardenia and cried, "MY PLANTS, MY PLANTS, WHERE ARE MY PLANTS?"

Her cry was so loud that she woke up all the animals. They rushed to her house and showed her the greenhouse.

Molly viewed the greenhouse by moonlight and thought it was beautiful. "I know my plants will be happy here," she said.

To show her gratitude, Molly decided to have a party for her friends. She sent out invitations.

*You are cordially invited
to my greenhouse party.
Come as your favorite plant.
Your friend,
Molly Patch*

When Goose got her invitation, she told Molly that she wished Chicken wasn't going to be at the party.

And when Chicken received her invitation, she told Molly that she wished Goose wouldn't attend the party.

On the day of the party, the greenhouse was crowded with all sorts of plants. Everyone was having fun. Molly went around with big platters of food. "I'm feeding my animal plants," she giggled.

The philodendron got along so well with the grape ivy that they spent the entire time at the party together. When it was time to remove masks, everyone laughed when it was discovered that the philodendron and grape ivy were Chicken and Goose.

Chicken and Goose didn't think it was so funny.

At first they shouted, "We've been tricked!"

But all the animals said it was a good trick.

Chicken and Goose agreed, and they hugged each other and thanked Molly Patch.

Molly thanked all the animals for the wonderful greenhouse. "I like it so much," she said, "I just might move in here."

"Oh, no!" The animals cried.

Molly smiled and began to water her piggybacks.

A Page From Molly's Notebook

the
greenhouse
is like
a
glass umbrella
when
the rain
touches
it

A NEW FRIEND

Clouds covered the moon. It was hard to tell what was real and what was shadow. It was the kind of night that makes you listen for sounds.

Molly Patch was in bed reading, and she listened. She heard an unfamiliar sound. It wasn't from the attic or the cellar, where strange sounds often come from. It was an outside sound.

Molly got out of bed to investigate. Outside, a spot of white moved between the shadows. At first it was difficult for Molly to make out what it was. She thought something had fallen from the sky.

When her eyes got used to the darkness, Molly was able to see a white cat. "Hello there!" she called out. "Are you lost?"

At first the cat didn't answer, but when Molly asked again, he answered, "Yes, I am!"

"Come inside. I'll put the kettle on," said Molly. "We'll have some warm milk."

The white cat didn't move. "Aren't you coming? Wouldn't you like something to eat?" asked Molly.

"Yes, I would like something to eat," said the cat.

"Come inside then," said Molly.

The cat moved slowly. Molly held the door open. "Is something the matter?" she asked.

The cat looked up at Molly. "I promised myself I would never do this again, but I am hungry," he said.

"Do what again?" asked Molly.

"Get involved with people," said the cat.

"Don't you trust me?" asked Molly.

"The last people I trusted took me for a long ride and left me in the woods. That's how I got here," said the cat.

"Oh dear!" cried Molly. "I'll prepare some nice cereal and you can tell me all about it."

After finishing two bowls of cereal with plenty of cream, the cat told Molly about his awful experiences with people. "It doesn't seem as if they care very long," said Cat.

"That isn't true of all people," said Molly. "You can stay with me."

"For how long?" asked Cat.

"For as long as you like!" answered Molly.

The cat followed Molly Patch upstairs and fell asleep at her feet. Molly smiled happily, and more than once she woke up to look at the cat. He didn't move.

The next day, the cat helped Molly with her chores. In the evening, when Crow stopped by to chat with Molly Patch, he was surprised by her new guest.

"This is Cat," said Molly, "and he is going to live with me."

Crow's visit was short. Molly was surprised, because usually he liked to stay and chat for a while.

Three days passed since Cat's arrival, and Molly thought it odd that she hadn't seen any of her friends.

"Something strange is going on," Molly said. And she went to the meadow, taking Cat along.

She ran through the meadow, calling the animals, but there wasn't any sign of them. Then she spotted Rabbit as he was about to jump over the stone fence. "Rabbit, what's going on? Where is everyone?" Molly cried.

There was a long silence. Then Rabbit said, "When we heard that you had a cat to live with, we figured that you didn't need us as friends anymore."

"Nonsense!" said Molly. "Now you tell everyone to come to my house this afternoon." Molly Patch returned home with the cat.

That afternoon all the animals visited Molly. "What sillies you are!" she told them. "Just because I find a new friend, it doesn't mean that I don't want my old ones. I love you all!"

Then Molly Patch introduced all the animals to Cat, and they exchanged stories with each other.

The animals told Cat about living in the forest, and he told them about living with people.

"I'd rather live in the forest," said Raccoon.

"I like living with Molly," said Cat.

"There's very little difference," said Bear.

Everyone laughed. That night Bear, Cat, Chicken, Crow, Field Mouse, Fox, Goose, Mole, Owl, Porcupine, Rabbit, Raccoon, Snake, Toad, and Woodpecker sat around and listened as Molly Patch told a story.

"There was once this little girl who lived in the city. But when the noises grew too loud and friendly faces disappeared, she moved to the country. . . ." Molly Patch began.

A Page From Molly's Notebook

fireflies dancing
through a summer night haze
putting on a show
for me
and my friends

Format by Kohar Alexanian

gr 2-4